MIRROR OF A HEALING SOUL

By Srishti Jain

A poetic journey from pain and hurt to learning, realization, and healing

PAPER TOWNS
PUBLISHERS

First Published by
Paper Towns Publishers
72, Vishwanath Dham Colony,
Niwaru Road, Jhotwara,
Jaipur, 302012

Mirror of a healing soul

ISBN Print Book - 978-93-6185-092-9

Printed in India

CONTENT

INTRODUCTION

This book is not only a collection of poetry, but a journey of how we feel and deal with our negative emotions, and learn and heal from them. It tries to help and remind each of the beautiful souls in pain that there is still hope left and chances available that could be taken to move forward in their life. "In darkness, we shine bright" is not just a proverb. If one reads this book, then there are chances that one would at least feel good or happy about oneself. Let's keep all the judgement about oneself aside and try to read as well as feel the words of this poetry. Each poetry is based on different emotions and pain and how one reaches from the bottom-line to realization and healing from the pain.

EMOTIONAL HEALING FROM OPPRESSION

THE GLASS CHARIOT

Keeping your feelings aside,

Moving with the forces back and side

Someone forcing you, to run fast for their ride

You are in speed, but your heart denies

You seem confused, but not surprised

But, you don't see your blessings are in disguise

Because you are not made for the horse race

Instead whatever you have, do embrace

Believe yourself, you are not a disgrace

Everybody runs for a living here

Do show some self-care

Not only your body, but your soul is also rare

You are ignoring the small huts

Because you are still pulling the glass chariot

See the lights when you pass by the colonies

Do see the beautiful sceneries

I know that the pulling of strings from behind hurts

But don't forget, it's you who pulls the glass chariot

Without you, the masters would be none

So, embrace yourself with a little grace

Your masters already are fighting for your stables, steads, and hay

EMOTIONAL HEALING FROM EMOTIONAL ABUSE

A FACADE SMILE

It's been a while, now it's time to laugh out loud

I was thinking *Am I that weird?* while walking in the crowd

Oh I can do this! But actually can I?

Thoughts meddling in my mind; no I am not shy

Yesterday, when I was standing up front

I was having faith and trust

But there were people, who were telling me

You are a disgust!

There were so many, so is that true?

Or my loved one said so, do I approve?

Well, naïve was I to believe their belief of mine!

Since then, I am walking with a facade smile

But now, the damage and this baggage is worthless

Because I am about to spread my wings, to glide like a butterfly!

Those whines made me wise

Those shouts made me realize

I am the one who can do it, and they are the ones with fake paradise

Oh, now I can't stop, because now is the start

This realization is now going to take me a thousand miles forward

Could it be that you all didn't want to see me succeed?

Because your hearts met with some greed?

It may be the greed of power

Or the greed of satisfaction

Or it could be your pain reliever by putting out absurd actions

But, let me tell you that there is damage you caused

And now, after a long time, let me put it to a pause

Because now is the time for a new life

My butterfly wings are going to make me flutter and rise

The sun, the stars and the sky are beautiful

Because now I see rainbows after your thrown arrows

EMOTIONAL HEALING FROM BODY SHAMING

THE BRUTAL APPEARANCE

Oh, I was tense!

My thoughts around my body were condensed

Those stinky feelings of unworthy style were my sense

But, little did I know, all these were nonsense

I heard from the whispers around me

Did this insecurity actually find me?

Oh lord! When will I unwind myself?

Does my appearance define me?

The less they saw, the more I cried

I have a heart of gold, but why do I get denied?

Because what they accepted was my appearance

It was like I was stuck at the door of the entrance

Well, long after I see and I sigh

Thank God that I have thrived

We can push ourselves through the entrance
And slam the doors of those whispers
Whatever others said, I denied

We fight the unseen battles
And speak our might
We come out of the appearance coma
Into the attractiveness flight

Yes, attitude and gratitude matter
Yes, being healthy and fit is for our own stride
The rest are only whispers
Because, guess what?
We fight, we survive, and we take our pride!

So, getting up with a broken heart, but not the limb
And breaking all the stereotypes
Those walking whispers of shaming
Can have rest or be in their own world
Because now, we have the power of our might

EMOTIONAL HEALING FROM GETTING IGNORED BY OTHERS

THE IGNORED SUNSHINE

Yes we cried, yes we whined

But all our emotions got declined

We didn't know the reason at all behind

They were closing their eyes, and moving away from the hind

"Oh, what have I done to you?" is all we ask!

But little do we know about their ego behind their mask

That ego killed our self-worth and left us to cry and whine

But little do they know that we are the child of divine

Yes, we question a lot about why we are ignored

But then we started to look at the sunshine

All our self-worth came back rushing to us

Do you know the reason behind?

Because, the sunshine is hid by the clouds

Like our self-esteem is hidden by ignorance

And that's when we realize that the sun still never ceases to shine

So let's get up and have a solo time

This time includes all the plans that we have

And the hard work that we do

So, now we walk alone by choice, not chance

And let others play their peek-a-boo!

EMOTIONAL HEALING FROM BEING AN OPTION

THE LAST AVAILABLE POSSIBILITY

We heard we are the only one
If they are sky, then we are their sun
Oh, the feeling that we got!
We are the only one that they thought

Keeping our energy aside
We were making sure that they stride
We kept on giving love in the house, where we thought we reside

Their bag was already filled with jewels for use
Still, they chose us and others were refused?
But then we see when jewels are of no use and not for free

Their empty bag is filled by a ruby
That ruby is costly and still here in their bag
And that they can use even without a price tag

Jewels are there on the top shelf of their slides
And next to them is an option where the ruby resides
But now we got tired of being a ruby for free
Because we know our worth and our energy

If kept on top, then we will still think
Because we are not an option, but a priority
We are enough to have our own bag in which we are studded
We don't need to be in other's bag that is already mudded
And here we are with our own self and shine!
Because we have our own light which is quite divine

EMOTIONAL HEALING FROM LOW SELF-CONFIDENCE

FROWNING EYES INSIDE

Walking down the stairs in the hall near the stage

Looking at others dancing with happiness, with their dreams to chase

Well, last night I imagined myself dancing free

I was looking so attractive like a flower surrounded by honey bees

Alas! That was just a dream

My voice is now having to scream

I can do it! I can dance!

I can sing, let's give it a chance!

The stage is all set, and it can be yours

Just go forward and break that silence of yours

Then, a voice came running and shouting, "STOP!"

"What if you don't know actually how to do it, you have to drop."

Your mind dwells with endless self-criticism

This is not made for you! You had better find a new vision

I was not so much afraid of the talent failures, should have kept that aside
I was less daring because of my own mind, giving me frowning eyes inside

Now I realize that it was just an illusion
An illusion that I am not perfect to be in that position
The stage is still all mine, only, if I accept it
Accepting my talents would let me fly higher
And now I am ready to set the stage on fire

I will no longer belittle my talents
It's a gift, so I will sharpen and make it in balance
I will dance and be free
No matter what days take me to be on stage
Well, it's time now to unfold my mystery!

EMOTIONAL HEALING FROM FEAR

THE BURNING CANDLE

I saw things coming towards me

The things that I like

These things were like a real deal to me

If done right, I would be surprised by life

I used my logic and saw the outcomes

I heard people around me who advised me to deny

My inner self was like a burning candle

It was just the fear that I couldn't handle

I wanted to try those opportunities with risk

What I saw and focused on was only the risk

The fear that I instilled with low self-esteem

Asking myself only the questions like, "What if I lose the stream?"

Didn't give those opportunities a chance

Because I instilled fear in advance

Fear of their perception, fear of being hurt
Fear that didn't sound good and sometimes even felt absurd

Now, I am ready to come out of those fears,
Because I had enough of here and there
This fear cannot make me procrastinate
Because I will take this leap of faith

I no longer will fear failure in advance
Because I won't feel guilty of failing without giving a chance
I am tired of this fear as my ambassador
I am breaking these walls with glass doors

Yes, goals are hard to reach and that's why they are our goals
But we shouldn't be so stuck in holes
I will try to reach and won't listen to those who say you can't
Because tried and tested is the best way we can grant

Sometimes we succeed, sometimes we fail
But we don't let this fear keep us trapped in our mental jail

We take steps for what is right

Yes, it takes a little push to try

So, let's give this push to ourselves

And try to test our tracks

Let's not think about the outcome and focus on what we do

Leave your destiny to God

Because he knows who you are and what you will do

EMOTIONAL HEALING FROM CONSTANT NEED FOR APPROVAL

THE EMPTY COLOSSEUM

We walk, we run, we fall and cry

We look around for someone to pick us up and sigh!

We can get up on our own

But that thought, we deny

Because all we want is someone giving us a hand and company besides

We walked down the empty Colosseum

Holding their hands

Why do we ask them where to even sit, and where to stand?

We laughed and cried as they said,

"Are our emotions dead?"

Then one day, we realize

Our own emotions are there, quite a surprise

Some happy, some sad

That does not mean that our emotions are bad

As we defend those emotions and not embrace

We create our own self as a following disgrace

Why did we need others' approval for everything?

Didn't our emotions tell us something?

But now, as we realize

We won't always need others' approval to survive

We will embrace our emotions and survive

Because we have someone special to ask and be our guide

That someone is us, as we are our best guide

Let's guide ourselves when in darkness,

And not only take us towards light, but also let's be the light!

EMOTIONAL HEALING FROM HOPELESSNESS

THE WITHERED SAND

Have you ever seen a beautiful desert?

And felt like you were withered sand?

Have you ever seen a rainbow?

And felt distinct from the colors that you could see and know?

We have to run towards the butterflies that we can't catch

Still, sometimes we have to adjust among people who we can't match

Our soul screams from inside, "Why are you sitting here and what are you doing?"

Is this the truth about yourself that you are pursuing?

Sometimes this makes us breakdown completely

It makes us feel to leave everything behind and run for relief

But, then something from inside shouts at us,

"Wait, hang in there, you are about to remove the thrust.

You are about to win over the curse, don't give up now.

There's a reason that you are here and now.

Find out the possibilities from it.

Sometimes the most difficult road is the one you have to take in."

Then, we get up and remove our tears

We gulp all the harsh words, and hardships, and all our fears

We have to flap our wings before we fly

Sometimes this flapping can be hurtful, but just don't deny

Yes we deserve love, life, and all the light

But, it's just a phase of a dark tunnel and we are at the end of the line

And we should trust us that everything will be fine

EMOTIONAL HEALING FROM COMPARISON

THE BACKYARD FLOWER

Day after day

Hour after hour

I see the garden growing

But, I am a backyard flower

Can't be seen, though beautiful I am

Do I belong to the garden?

Or is the backyard where I stand?

I saw the winds flowing, both in the garden and here

If that wind is the same

The gardener is the same

The soil is the same

Then, why am I here?

Well, once I shouted and asked those flowers of the garden,

"Why are you all there? Excuse me, pardon!"

They replied, "How precious you are.

The owner keeps you especially in the backyard.

He sits there and stares.

He takes care of you more than us, we think."

I told them, "I am alone, and you all have each other, don't you all think?"

But then, I realized

Why am I doubting myself?

They are there with all the beauty for a garden

And I am me, the pearl of the warden!

We all are different, with different styles

We all have different abilities, but with dazzling smiles

Some are front, some are back and yet to be seen

Maybe that's the reason why sometimes people are mean

We all have beauty, some are intelligent, and some are free

So, I stopped looking at the flowers that are together

And I started looking at the attention from the owner

I felt happy for them and even for me

Maybe more than me, they needed the company

The universe has a method to balance

The rest is your way of thinking to enhance

I might be sad if I compare

So, let's go with my own unique adventure

With our own lovely fare

I make friends with the flowers of the garden

Because now, I understand them and their prayers

I stopped comparing and got compassion and care

EMOTIONAL HEALING FROM ANGER

TWO SIDE WEAPON

Why am I agitated?

What is the reason?

Shall I shut my mouth and wait for the treason?

My eyes got red

There are thoughts in my head

My patience all tested

Now, those bizarre words rested

Rested on someone who made me move

Well, now the reason came to lose my groove

Whether I should hit or abuse them

But wait, by doing this will I lose them?

They were harsh on me, why can't I?

Well, that's the difference between them and me

I can't let their words and actions agitate me

Let them love or hate me

Let's not give them a reason to be hurt by me
Because that's what my anger will make me see
This will destroy my little heap of heaven
Just like a two-way weapon

This sudden pent-up rage and agitation
Looks satisfying if thrown back to the giver
But, it's temporary and a waste of passion

We lose our minds as if we're so weak
As if someone has the right on us to be meek
Well, it's the power that we give to others, to make us hurt and do things
It would be much better, if their words and actions didn't give them a thing

Better to not act because of others' words, thoughts, and redemptions
It's not what we are and neither do we defend our feelings against them
So let's stop taking their harshness and words to heart
And stop this scam

EMOTIONAL HEALING FROM EMOTIONAL DEPENDENCY

THE EMPTY HOLLOWS

Wherever I went, it followed

I shouted from inside, "Will this hurt or give me sorrow?"

I looked around to cling to making decisions

Only to cover my false precisions

The tale was never-ending, but I tried

I tried to find people who would accept or deny

I got a few to whom I gave the power

Without realizing my empty self-devour

I felt happy when they said yes or no

I felt confident when they told me to wait or go

I started to doubt every of my decisions

Self-criticism and avoiding emotions became my optimism

But we come to a point where we can't avoid

The people around use our acceptance and fill their own void

We gave them the power to handle on their own

But, now since the job went wrong

Time for our return!

We need to realize our own power

The power to withstand when we accept our emotions and positions

We shouldn't let our emotions go on tour

And let self-criticism and failures destroy our core

We shouldn't let others decide for us

So that we enjoy our problem-solving escapism

We should stand in our power and accept the situation

We will know our limitless might

Accepting our emotions and learning will bring us our own sights

The directions that we think others would give us

Without us being there are right

Will just create fogs in the night

So let us face our own sentiments and directions

'Cause we are the creator of our inner happiness and infatuations

A JUMBLE BOX

Our lives are going to different paths
We don't know if something ever lasts
But there is a constant flow of thought
That we couldn't unwind
Some twisted, some unwanted
Some beautiful and wanted

But this thinking is not getting to halt
It's like our mind is tasting pepper and salt
We got so habituated to this mirage of the mind
That we forgot our being and kind

These thoughts are getting on our nerves
We are the victims that it serves
We cry and laugh
We wish and deny
Sometimes, we even try to defy

Well, why don't we sit thoughtless for some time?

Let us give it a try to relax our mind

Let's try to find out who we are without these overflowing thoughts

Let's not try to always pull out socks

Because our life is not a jumble box

It doesn't mean to avoid your intuitions

All it means is to stop the overflowing situations

Sometimes let your-self have a lullaby

Because this time, these unnecessary thoughts have to pass by

EMOTIONAL HEALING FROM EMOTIONAL SENSITIVITY

A SHOWER SPONGE

Yes, we know that we are sad

We know they could be bad

We thought we get the reason

But our thoughts are changing like the changing seasons

We say we get why they are mad

We get all our sick emotional threads

Why do we feel so much pleasure and pain

While our innermost happiness goes down in the drain?

We look at ourselves from two mirrors

One of our pain and one of their critique fear

Why don't we start looking at a new page

A page filled with our own awareness

But it has our whole stage

A page where our true happiness and compassion is written

A page where we know what they think and sometimes it is not belittled?

We need to know who we truly are and what we want
Before directly coming to the conclusions of pain haunts
We don't need to just notice their behavior from dusk 'till dawn
Don't suck the upper layer of emotions like a shower sponge

We need to look at how we behave and pay attention
No need to deny or justify our rights and passions
We can just confront our poor behavior
And make ourselves our own friends first
Now, let's go to the relationship endeavors!

EMOTIONAL HEALING FROM SELF VICTIMIZATION

THE BURNING FOREST

Last time I cried, again I denied
Well, it's not my fault, it is their revolt
I felt like all is against me
Why has the outside world chained me?

Why don't I get the kind of people I want to be with?
Because my situation makes me miserable in widths
Why am I an object to be targeted?
I have lost something again, I bet

It's totally not my fault
People I know are the ones who put salt
Why didn't I get a better place to be happy?
'Cause everyone around me behaves crappy
They smile and laugh at each other, but why not me?
Am I that invisible to be?

But then, I told myself, "Stop this!
You yourself are going to flop this.
Why are you always condemning others and the condition?
Maybe it is your inner awareness at an unhealthy disposition."

"Yes, the situation maybe is not good and a little bit off,
But why to blame it on the whole world, please stop!"
Yes, I came out of the pain and hesitation
So let's pat my back for the great redemption."

I say 'you' all the time, but is it me who whines.
Shouldn't I be thankful to gain so much strength?
Because something inside me is changing and should be new brand
Can I be thankful for the things I get?
Because when there are storms, I only get wet.

Whoever the people are, whatever the situation is
I should know how to keep myself in bliss
I should at least try to make my own self happy
Without blaming others' behavior towards me

Because at the end, the change to resist is going to be made by me

I should not let others' behavior and situations define me

And be responsible for my own self inside me.

EMOTIONAL HEALING FROM REJECTION

ACCESS DENIED

So many times your heart cried
It's like you waited for your delivery, but it didn't arrive
You have overpaid the price
But still, you got "access denied"

You know the place whether work or their heart
You wished you were chosen for the position from the start
Alas, you tried and tried
Now, your tears are also dried

The numbness you felt from the unhealed wounds
Now the time has come to make your ground
You are realizing that it sucks to just lay down and sit
You were born to rise like a phoenix!

Yes, you heard this in your head and heart, and it is right
Because you learned your lesson, with this, your future will be bright

With the pain of refusals, you collected

The work you didn't get, your chance in love rejected

Now, you are ready to make a garland of your pain

And let your confidence be attracted

Wear your pain like a necklace, don't let it be a rope that chokes you

Let the necklace shine bright and get up with the newfound hope too

Those refusals were meant to give you power and direction

To build confidence in yourself for your next preferred big destined selection

This selection you will get with the newfound confidence and power

That you got from the determined rejections from wrong directions

EMOTIONAL HEALING FROM FEAR OF FAILURE

THE FALLING CARDS

Oh, we tried so hard!
But thrown back with a double-punch
We got up again
And someone knocked us down in the sun

Our falling again and again
Each time hits us so hard
Our enthusiasm went down the drain
It seemed like falling cards

The more we got thrown
The more came worries of the unknown
We saw failure at every door
That's the reason we chose to ignore
Ignoring the changes and opportunities that we saw
Because of the unbearable pain of failing to be

Why give up without even trying?

Let's not give in to a series of crying

I know that it is hard to bear the pain

But why feel drenched without getting in the rain?

There are a hundred ways and a thousand varieties

Let us try them all and see what is best for you and me

For some, they get their variety soon and some late

But don't stop trying all the plates

What is made for you will definitely come by

But all you gotta do is try and again try

We failed not one, but many times

But it is the satisfaction that we get when at least we try

We learn and grow and then fly high

So take it as the growth and do pass by

Maybe we fail again

But the world knows our efforts and somewhere it won't go down the drain

Let's try again and see

Maybe the next variety is our real place to be!

The clothes we try fail to fit

But we do try different clothes until we look lit!

In the same way, let's walk the path, don't sit back and crawl

Let's just be a wolf, once stopped, then again we howl

EMOTIONAL HEALING FROM OVER SELF-CRITICISM

ROADS OF MIRAGE

We usually open our mind's garage

So that we could ask

Why did I do wrong?

Can I compensate for my part?

Yes, it is good to learn from our mistakes

And let us reconnect from the start

It's good to sometimes sit and ponder on oneself

It's pretty good art!

But, do we sit and always point fingers at ourselves?

When our fault is not there itself

Do we raise only high expectations from us?

And then forget to enjoy our success for us?

Yes, we should ponder and compensate for our mistakes

But we should not always put our being at stake?

We should know that somewhere we are wrong

But don't forget the places where we are right

Because we win and loose with all our might

Let's do what we want with whatever we learned

Then witness, acknowledge, and remember

If we did something wrong

Then we can surrender

Or else, let's move forward

With happiness and whatever we enjoyed

Because with the teachings

We can definitely spread happiness inside-out, and joy!

THE MISSING CARRIAGE

Tell us where you all are

Tell us how you have been

Why are we suffering to just see a glimpse of you all?

Why haven't you ever seen it?

Yes, now to we laugh and cry

Because since you left, our tears are dry

We tried to find you all in our hearts, they say it is easy

But all we do is stop thinking about you all

And keep ourselves busy

Our days passing by

The things that we learned, we still try

Thinking about you all makes us sigh

It seems like we are running towards an empty stage

The destinations we want to reach, but it's the missing carriage

We shouldn't feel that empty inside
We should not feel heavy, just because we have crossed a bumpy ride
Yes they are not here and only their memory surrounds
But do not forget their vision and bounds

Yes, there is no comeback for the ones who left
But that's definitely sure that they wouldn't want us to live in memory debt
They would like us to just remember them
And we go to our destinations
Because we shouldn't miss the trains at the stations

Yes, they were too important for us to leave
But all they want us to just move on with the belief
And as we understand this and move with what further we perceive
That's when we start to get relief

COLD WINDS

I trusted people with my heart and mind
My dreams were joined with theirs for grind
My expectations were reaching heights
I was fixing my own rights

We know when our efforts go in vane
The trust was broken and I stood in pain
Their mighty words as if they are fairies
In the end, some are really scary

I thought that their promises wouldn't be skimmed
But here I was, standing alone in cold winds
I thought that I would fall and cry
My trembling knees and teary eyes
I wanted some medicine or redemption
So that I could trust others again without tension

But gradually, I understood the rules of this game

We might face situations that are the same

We shouldn't feel dejected and give the pressure of expectations to others

If one breaks the trust, there must be a faithful another

Even if there is no one around to trust again

One powerful trustworthy is our own heart and brain

So don't stand in the cold wind

And get up on your feet

Choose your support wisely from the previous lesson

Because now they won't be mean or a cheat

Yes, we are stabbed at the heart

But, don't let our hearts die

Let them beat again

Because, in the night, glow the fireflies

EMOTIONAL HEALING FROM DISCRIMINATION

TWISTED DIRECTIONS

We were in the place, where we lost our reflection
Our broken pieces were trying to have perfection
The mere mirage of us being better and to be seen
Was all we needed to be chosen as a better option

We forgot that there are some set standards for them
Those standards are the broken myth and hard for us to understand
They say they choose because we are not the ones to use
Is there any issue with us, then why should we lose?

They see the other one perfect, they care about them
Then, why are we standing in place like a broken lamb?
They tell us to be like the other
Well, we should make them proud like no other

But then, we realize
That their appreciation, care, and affection will cost us a prize

That prize is to mold ourselves to their standards

Why put ourselves in a situation where we get cliffhangers?

We deserve that love and devotion for our own authenticity

And the love that the other one gets is the matching of standards for some not me

So, let's tell ourselves, "My love, let it be.

We Are not the chosen assets to match their kind of reliability."

Our worth and magic will be chosen by someone else

For them, we won't be less

Different likings and a different mess

So, why take the stress?

We should not pay attention to the chosen attractions

We are different flavors with different additions and subtractions

So, if another one receives more than us from them

Then don't sit in dejection

Let's take the walk to our own destination

Walking for their affection will lead us to twisted directions

EMOTIONAL HEALING FROM WORTHLESSNESS

A TORN PAGE

I looked at my ground and stage
I thought about my qualities and age
Oh! I contemplated on my achievements
I thought less of gains and more of pains

What did I do that all these years?
Where will I go with the collected fears?
What if I vanish, will someone cry?
Will someone call me, or is there no try?

I thought that I am not a jack of all trades and a master of none
Oh, what can I do with my life, there is still no sun
But then I realized, life is beyond my known capacity and age
So, why sit and dust myself like a torn page?

Yes, I still got hurt and it made feel directionless
But this didn't stop me to explore the mess

Situations might still mock us, but remember it's a test

Because sometimes how we get up is the real awareness

We fell, we learned, we got up and walked

We walked forward, leaving the bad experiences and taking the lessons with us

We learn and learn and evolve within

But that evolution is not seen with service and monetary biddings

As we get strong and free from stress in this mess

That's when we become a complete page without really being worthless

We may temporarily feel low with the stealthy situation

But we should again glow with the learning from hesitation

This is not a stop of our worth

This is just a new start of a new learning

And our evolution takes further birth

EMOTIONAL HEALING FROM INSECURITY

THE FALLING TREE

Oh! My gown is so beautiful, but does it suit me?
They say that my smile is pretty, but is it really what they see?
I think I might lose whatever is left in me
My eyes glimmered with hope, but the brightness is now withering

My life felt constrained, but they saw me free
Things seemed out of control for me
My pride and aim are high like a tall tree
But my insecurity made my aims fall down like a falling tree

I thought in self-doubt, "What if I lose the precious things?
What if I cut my solid wings?"
But then, something called me from inside
"Why are you feeling dim, when actually you can shine bright?
Your own possessions won't go anywhere
Your relations are what they and your heart adheres."

My answers came from my outer glow

Which came out when I saw the actual beautiful show

A show where I am what I don't see, I am young at heart, wild and free

I don't need to have second thoughts

My love and life are around and will not be lost

I don't need to feel tied to "What if?" and "I am not so sure."

All I need is to be happy, have trust in my qualities, and my nature

ACKNOWLEDGEMENT

A book contains not only the efforts of the writer but also the confidence, well wishes, support, and contributions of the loved ones. Therefore, I would like to thank my friends, family, and well-wishers who deeply motivated me and assisted me to write this book. No book is complete without its cover. So, I also would like to thank my brother, Videh Jain, for helping me with the cover of my book. Special thanks to Ahmed Saffu for the cover image. I also would like to thank the future readers who would appreciate my heart and work through this book.